A PIG, A FOX, AND STINKY SOCKS

For Mima, Papa, Grandma, and Grandpa—JF

PENGUIN WORKSHOP
An Imprint of Penguin Random House LLC, New York

Copyright © 2017 by Jonathan Fenske. All rights reserved. Previously published in 2017 by Penguin Young Readers. This paperback edition published in 2019 by Penguin Workshop, an imprint of Penguin Random House LLC, New York. PENGUIN and PENGUIN WORKSHOP are trademarks of Penguin Books Ltd, and the W colophon is a registered trademark of Penguin Random House LLC. Manufactured in China.

Visit us online at www.penguinrandomhouse.com.

Library of Congress Control Number: 2016048030

ISBN 9780593095973   10 9 8 7 6 5 4 3

A PIG, A FOX, AND STINKY SOCKS

by Jonathan Fenske

Penguin Workshop

PART ONE

5

And hide inside
this handy pail.

LAUNDRY

To watch Pig find
his stinky mail.

LAUNDRY

8

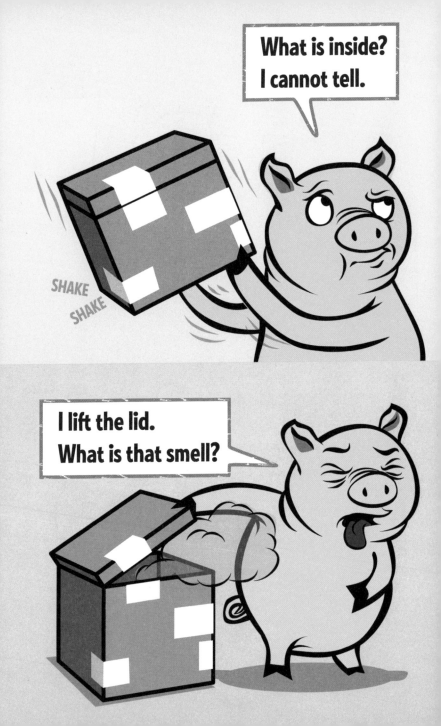

12

PART TWO

18

Another pair of socks that stink.
Another funny trick I think.

27

PART THREE

32